CHOOSE YOUR OWN ADVENTURE®

Fans Love Reading
Choose Your Own Adventure®!

"Come on in this book if you're crazy enough!
One wrong move and you're a goner!"
Ben Curley, Age 9

"They have a mystery to them that makes it fun to read.
I like being able to solve them my own way."
Gabe Pibril, Age 10

"Sometimes I'm scared because I
don't know what will happen. Then I just
make a different choice."
Natasha Burbank, Age 9

"If you want to go on a magnificent adventure
of your choice, go to page 1 and begin reading.
If you don't then get another book!"
Quillyn Peterson, Age 9

Illustrated by: Keith Newton
Book and cover design by: Julia Gignoux, Freedom Hill Design and Book Production

For information regarding permission, write to:

CHOOSECO
P.O. Box 46
Waitsfield, Vermont 05673
www.cyoa.com

A DRAGONLARK BOOK

ISBN: 1-933390-52-2
EAN: 978-1-933390-52-9

Published simultaneously in the United States and Canada

Printed in Canada

0 9 8 7 6 5 4

CHOOSE YOUR OWN ADVENTURE®

Your Very Own ROBOT

BY R. A. MONTGOMERY

ILLUSTRATED BY KEITH NEWTON

A DRAGONLARK BOOK

A DRAGONLARK BOOK

To Shanny, Becca, Lila, and Avery

READ THIS FIRST!!!

WATCH OUT!
THIS BOOK IS DIFFERENT
than every book you've ever read.

Do not read this book from the first page
through to the last page.
Instead, start on page 1 and read until you
come to your first choice. Then turn to the
page shown and see what happens.

When you come to the end of a story,
you can go back and start again.
Every choice leads to a new adventure.

Good luck!

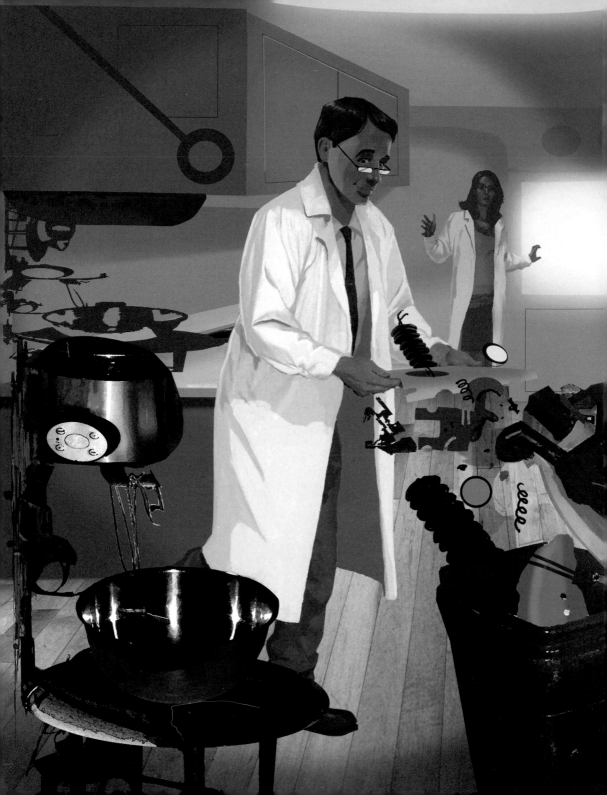

Everybody wants a robot. Only a few people get to have one. That's because robots are hard to make—and they also cost a lot of money.

You are one of the lucky ones who gets to own a robot. Here's how it happens:

Your mom and dad are scientists. They work with robots every day. Sometimes they even build them.

One day, they build a robot that seems to do everything wrong. "I've tried to fix it and I can't," your father says. So he tosses the robot into the trash.

Turn to page 2.

"Poor robot!" you say. "Mom and Dad gave up on you too fast. I think I can fix you up. I've seen them build lots of robots."

You collect nuts, bolts, some wire, and leftover computer parts. Bang! Twist! You work on your robot all day long. Soon it starts to look much better.

Turn to the next page.

"You look so good, I'm going to give you a name," you tell it. So you name your robot Gus.

"There's still more work," you tell your robot. "You could use a few coats of paint. But I'd really like to turn you on now and see what you can do."

Your robot should work just as well without paint, shouldn't it?

If you turn your robot on right away, turn to page 7.

If you paint him first, turn to page 9.

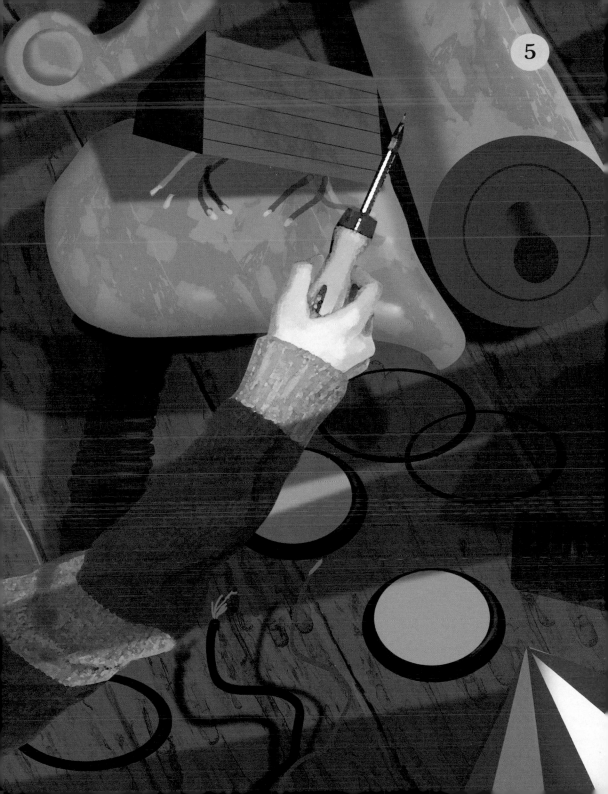

You turn your robot on. CLICK! He stands up! He sure is tall. Your robot flashes red and blue lights, and his eyes shine bright yellow. "BLOOP-DE-BEEP," he says, holding out his arms to you. "BLEEP-DO-DEEP. I'M ALL YOURS."

"Terrific!" you tell him. "Now I'll turn on your computer." BEEP! BUZZ!

"He works!" you shout. "I fixed him." Then you see a dial on the side of your robot. The dial has numbers from 1 to 100. A sign says: Turn the dial to your age. So you do.

Turn to the next page.

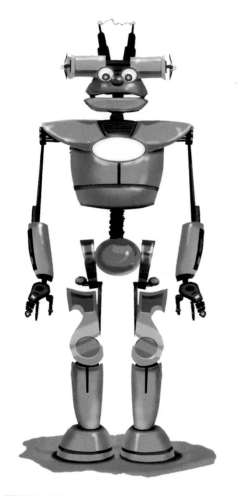

"BLEEP!" says your robot. "NOW I CAN TAKE YOU ON AN ADVENTURE THAT'S PERFECT FOR YOU."

You're not sure if you should go on any adventures yet. After all, you have never used a robot by your-self before.

If you switch him off and ask your parents how to work him, turn to page 12.

If you use your robot right away, turn to page 15.

You decide to paint your robot first. So you spray him with silver paint until he shines. Now you are ready to turn him on.

CLICK! "GLEEP! BEEP!" is the first thing he says. "I AM SO GLAD TO BE ON. PUT ME TO WORK AND SEE WHAT I CAN DO!"

Turn to the next page.

"I sure will," you tell him.

"FIRST I COULD USE A LITTLE MORE PAINT ON MY BACK," he says.

"OK," you say. You spray a lot more paint on him.

"MEEP! IT TICKLES!" your robot yells. He laughs so hard that he falls down and rolls around in the mud.

"Oh, no!" you groan. "Now I have to clean you up."

"NOPE, NEEP!" your robot says. "I CAN WORK JUST AS WELL IF I AM DIRTY."

Maybe he can, but he looks terrible!

If you let him stay muddy, turn to page 22.

If you wash your robot, turn to page 24.

You ask your mom and dad how to work your robot. They show you all his special knobs and buttons. "Have fun!" says your mother.

"But be careful," warns your father. "Some of your robot's buttons may not work correctly."

Then they drive off to go shopping.

Turn to page 14.

14

"I think I will press this button that says SING," you say.

WHOOSH! Your robot starts to steam. "No, SING!" you yell.

But he is doing it all wrong. Clouds of steam are rising from him. Is he going to take off like a rocket? Yes!

Now what do you do? Should you hop on him? Or should you call the fire department to rescue him?

If you leap on your robot, turn to page 28.

If you call the fire department, turn to page 30.

You want to use your robot right away. First you take him out and introduce him to your friends. "I want you to meet my robot, Gus," you tell them. "I fixed him myself!"

Turn to page 59.

You want to see if your robot can fly. You press his RUN button twice, hoping he will take off like a jet. Instead of flying, your robot leaps into the high telephone wires.

Go on to the next page.

"I'll save you!" you say. You grab a rope and lasso him.

"WOOPY MOOP!" says your robot. "I DID NOT DO THAT VERY WELL."

"You sure didn't," you say. "I'm never going to press your RUN button again!"

"Now it's time to go to school," you say.

"I'M NOT PROGRAMMED TO GO TO SCHOOL," says your robot. "WHY NOT PRESS MY LASER BUTTON INSTEAD?"

That might be fun! It could also be dangerous. Maybe you should just take your robot to school.

If you take your robot to school, turn to page 62.

If you press his laser button, turn to page 64.

"Now, STOP!" you shout. But your robot keeps jumping.

"Come back!" you yell, chasing him.

Your robot jumps into an ice cream factory. He keeps jumping until he lands—in an enormous tub of strawberry ice cream!

Go on to the next page.

"GLUMP!" he yells. "I'M NOT PROGRAMMED TO SWIM."

You know how to swim. But the ice cream looks very cold and thick. What if you sink down in it—forever?

If you dive in to save your robot, turn to page 33.

If you yell for help, turn to page 38.

You land on Planet Silver, the robot planet.

You see thousands of robots, beeping and flashing. "WELCOME!" says the Robot King. "WE ARE GLAD YOU ARE HERE. YOU WILL STAY HERE FOREVER BECAUSE WE DON'T WANT EARTH TO KNOW ABOUT US."

"Why not?" you ask.

"BECAUSE THEY WILL MAKE US ALL WORK FOR THEM," says the king.

"I will keep your secret," you say.

"NOPE," says the Robot King. "YOU ARE STAYING WITH US."

When you look at your arms and legs you are stunned. You are turning into a robot!

"BLEEP! OOPS!" you say. "Goodbye Earth!"

The End

You let your robot stay muddy and take him for a walk in the neighborhood. Soon a crowd gathers around him.

A junk truck drives by. "Say," shouts the junk man, "that's a nice piece of scrap metal." He grabs your robot and tosses him into his truck.

"STOP!" you call. Too late!

The junk man gets into his truck. Luckily, somebody has called the TV station about your robot. A TV truck comes down the street.

Should you ask the TV truck to follow the junk truck? Or should you leap into the junk truck right now and rescue your robot by yourself?

If you leap into the junk truck, turn to page 26.

If you ask the TV truck to follow the junk truck, turn to page 66.

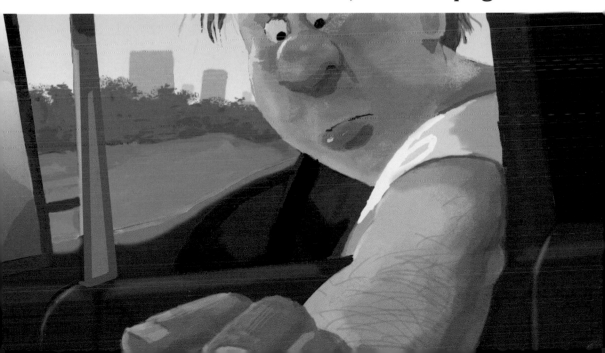

You wash the mud off your robot with the garden hose. Soon he is clean and shiny again.

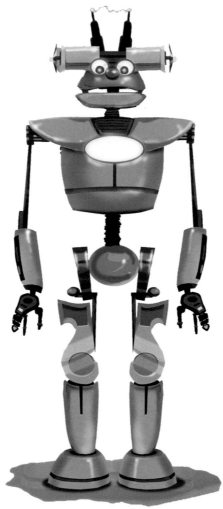

"Now I will try pressing your RUN button," you tell him. So you do—and off he runs.

"Terrific!" you cry, and you turn him off before he can run too far.

"Say, maybe if I let you run fast enough, you could take off, like a plane!" you say. "But, of course, I don't know how to fly a plane. So that might be dangerous."

"Besides, there are lots of things we could do in the yard. We could build a fort together. That would be fun."

But you keep thinking about flying. Should you try it? Or should you build the fort?

If you decide to build the fort, turn to page 35.

If you want to see if your robot can fly, turn to page 16.

"I must save my robot!" you yell as you leap into the junk truck. That makes the junk man very, very angry.

"Both of you are in serious trouble now!" he warns.

Go on to the next page.

When he gets to the junkyard, the junk man heads for a huge bucket loader.

"I am going to mash you and your robot to bits!" he screams.

"Get us out of this mess," you tell your robot, pressing his PROBLEM SOLVING button.

"BLEEP! MOOP!" he says. Your robot races the junk man to the bucket loader and gets there first. He scoops up the junk man and drops him onto a huge pile of garbage.

Turn to page 40.

You leap on your robot. Both of you blast into space. You go past Mars, past Jupiter, past the Milky Way!

Turn to page 21.

You call the fire department to rescue your flying robot. The firemen shoot a huge spray of water at him, and down he comes. "Are you hurt?" you ask, running over to your robot.

Go on to the next page

"PEEP, NOPE," he says. "BUT I CAN NEVER FLY AGAIN."

"That's sad," you tell him. "But, of course, you can still do lots of other things."

Turn to the next page.

"NO, NO!" sighs your robot. "I CAN'T. IF I CAN'T FLY, I DON'T WANT TO DO ANYTHING."

"That's terrible," you moan.

"THAT'S THE WAY I AM," says your robot. He sits down and clicks off. You try and try, but you can't turn him on again.

Maybe if you are patient, he will recharge and turn on again. Maybe.

The End

You dive into the strawberry ice cream to save your robot. "BRR, it's cold!" you shout. "But it tastes great!" You push your robot to safety.

"We'd better leave before somebody sees us," you tell him.

"OOP! YES!" he says. So you both run out the door and head for home. All your friends laugh when they see you. They grab spoons and try to scoop off some ice cream.

Turn to the next page.

"Let's take a warm shower," you say to your robot.

"NO THANKS!" he says. "I'LL RUST." He flashes a warm light beam at you, and you are dried instantly.

"Next time, try jumping into some hot fudge," you tell him. And both of you laugh.

Turn to page 48.

You decide to build a tree fort with your robot. "The maple tree looks best," you say.

"BLEEP!" he agrees.

"Bring me those old boards," you tell him. The two of you hammer and saw and build a wonderful fort.

Turn to page 37.

"I can see for miles!" you shout. Just then you see lightning flash, and you hear thunder roar and shake the earth. "Let's get out of here!" you yell.

Before you can climb down the tree, a bolt of lightning comes right at you. Your robot throws himself right in front of you. He saves your life! But the lightning strikes him.

"GEEP!" he says, and then he falls to the earth and clicks off.

Is he broken forever? Should you try to fix him, or should you wait to see if he wakes up?

If you wait to see if he wakes up by himself, turn to page 42.

If you try to fix him, turn to page 55.

"HELP!" you yell.

"ZEEP, ZOOP," your robot says as he sinks deeper into the strawberry ice cream.

The president of the ice cream factory comes running. He gets you a rubber raft and you jump on it. You row your robot back to safety.

Go on to the next page.

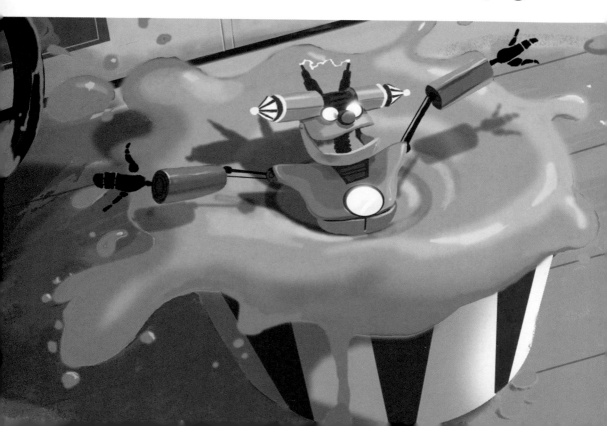

"BLOOP, EEP," he says. "THANKS!"

"That will be $800 for ruining my ice cream," says the president.

"But I don't have $800," you say.

"Then you must go to jail," says the president.

"OOP," whispers your robot. "PRESS MY ZIP BUTTON, AND I CAN GET US OUT OF HERE!"

But will he just get you deeper into trouble?

If you decide you'd better go to jail, turn to page 43.

If you press the robot's ZIP button, turn to page 45.

"That's what you get for stealing my robot," you call back to the junk man as you head home.

"What's for dinner tonight?" you ask your father when you get home.

"Leftovers," he says.

"Ecch. I'll skip it," you say. You eat fried pond scum—your very favorite dish!

The End

That night, your family watches the news together.

"There you are!" says your mother. "You look terrific."

"We're so proud of you," says your father.

The phone rings just then and you run to get it. "We want to do a story about you and your robot for our newspaper," says a reporter.

"Sure!" you say. You give your robot another paint job so that both of you will look terrific!

The End

Your robot looks like he's waking up.

"WOOP!" he says. "THAT LIGHTNING GAVE ME A BURST OF ENERGY! I'M READY TO FLY TO ANOTHER PLANET!" And off he goes! You grab onto his legs just in time, and you fly off with him.

"Let's go to Venus," you say.

"ROGER!" says your robot. And you fly fast through a haze of yellow light.

Turn to page 61.

The president of the ice cream factory takes you and your robot to jail.

"BOOP! I DON'T LIKE THIS PLACE," says your robot.

"Neither do I," you moan.

The jailer feeds you bread and water. Your robot gets oil.

"I wish I never fixed you," you say.

Turn to the next page.

"GLEEP! I WISH YOU HAD LEFT ME IN THE TRASH," groans your robot. "AT LEAST THE FOOD WAS GOOD."

You miss your family and your friends a lot. Day after day, you watch old robot shows on TV. "Never try to fix a broken robot," says a scientist.

"Now you tell me," you sigh.

One day your mother and father appear on the news. "That's my mother and father," you shout to the jailer.

"Sure, sure," he says.

The End

You press your robot's ZIP button. Suddenly, your robot shoots out paper. "NOW, PRESS MY PRINT BUTTON," he says. So you do. He starts printing out money! He prints out exactly $800.

Turn to the next page.

"Thanks," says the president of the ice cream factory. "Now, go away."

You run out, very happy. "What a great robot you are," you say. "You are going to print lots of money and make me rich."

"ZOOP! SORRY!" says your robot. "I ONLY PRINT MONEY ONCE EVERY HUNDRED YEARS."

"Why didn't you say that before?" you moan. You are so angry at your robot that you don't talk to him for the rest of the day.

Go on to the next page.

"Well, maybe I will never be rich," you say. "But at least I don't have to go to jail!"

The End

"You are my best friend," you say to your robot, and you give him a big hug.

"Now, I'm going to show you my favorite place of all."

You take your robot down to the ocean. "Look at all those ships," you say. "That ship looks very strange. Let's sneak onto it and see what's going on."

Go on to the next page.

Turn to the next page.

"OOP, DEEP!" says your robot as you climb aboard. "I'M PROGRAMMED TO SOLVE MYSTERIES."

Suddenly, the ship sails off. You are going to sea!

Turn to page 69.

"GOOD RIDDANCE," the pirates yell, as they push you off the plank.

SPLASH! BLEEP! You and your robot hit the water. The ship sails off.

"We're done for," you say.

"DEEPY, FREEP," your robot calls. "IT'S A GOOD THING I'M PROGRAMMED TO CALL WHALES."

"WHOOM!" he calls. And a huge whale leaps up from below.

"ZOOP!" says your robot. "CAN YOU GIVE US A LIFT?"

"WHOOM!" says the whale. And he rides you both back to shore.

"It's time you learned how to swim," you tell your robot. So you spend the rest of the day teaching him.

The End

You and your robot are going to fight the pirates. But how? "I will try pressing your SPIN button," you say. It works! Your robot spins so fast that he makes a huge wind. That huge wind blows all the pirates off the boat!

Turn to page 57.

"Poor robot," you groan. "I've got to bring you back to life."

You pick up your robot and stand him on his funny metal legs. He wobbles and falls down again—plunk! You get an idea.

You run back to the lab as fast as you can, and you look through your parents' special emergency repair kit. You grab one part and bring it back. Carefully you take off your robot's head and put the part right in the middle of his chest.

Turn to the next page.

Your robot's lights start to flash again. His arms and legs jerk, and he stands up!

"CLOSE CALL!" he says. "VERY CLOSE CALL!"

"I'm so glad you're OK," you shout. And you give him the biggest hug you can!

The rain has stopped and the sun is out again. You and your robot climb back up to your fort. You play there for the rest of the day.

The End

"Happy landings!" you yell. You radio the Coast Guard to pick up the pirates.

"You get a $5,000 reward for finding them," says the Coast Guard captain. "They are wanted for smuggling gold."

Turn to the next page.

"TERRIFIC!" you say. Then you turn to your robot. "I'm sure glad I fished you out of the trash, old Robo!"

"MEEP! ME TOO," says your robot. "BUT I WISH I HAD A FEW ROBOT FRIENDS."

So you use the reward money to make a few more robots. They keep your robot company when you are at school!

The End

"Show us!" they say. You press your robot's JUMP button. Your robot jumps six feet into the air.

Turn to page 18.

Venus is all soft and yellow and gooey, like half-melted cheese. The whole planet is like a huge amusement park!

You play all day, and then you fly home in time for dinner.

"How did your shoes get so sticky?" asks your father.

"I—uh, don't know," you answer.

"I DO!" laughs your robot from under the table. Quickly, you turn him off so he doesn't tell.

Nobody ever knows you really went to Venus!

The End

You take your robot to school. Of course, all the kids love him. "Can your robot clean out the wastebasket and pass out the chalk?" asks your teacher, Ms. Sims.

"Sure," you say, though you don't really know for sure. You press a few buttons and turn your robot loose. He picks up the wastebasket and dumps it on your teacher's desk!

Go on to the next page.

"STOP!" you yell. He doesn't! He takes the chalk and breaks it and throws it out the window!

Ms. Sims runs up to your robot and yells, "If you do not stop, I am going to make you stay after school and write 'I AM A BAD ROBOT' on the blackboard one thousand times."

"I AM NOT PROGRAMMED FOR THAT!" says your robot, and he runs out the door.

The next day you have to stay after school and write 'I AM A VERY BAD ROBOT TRAINER'—one thousand times!

Phooey!

The End

ZAP! You press the LASER button on your robot. A beam flashes. There's one thing wrong—the beam is aimed right at you! You leap up into the air and the beam misses you by an inch. But it burns down the rose bushes in Mr. Grump's garden!

The Grumps are roaring mad! They tell your mom and dad. You have to spend every day for a week planting new roses.

"SORRY! I AM NOT PROGRAMMED TO PLANT ROSE BUSHES," says your robot, and laughs.

You laugh too—because it is very funny!—not.

The End

"STOP!" you yell at the TV truck. You tell the cameraman about your robot. "A scoop!" he yells. "We will save your robot and show it on TV too!"

You all drive off after the junk man.

Suddenly, the junk truck comes to a red light. It stops so fast that the TV truck bumps into it. Your robot flies into the air!

You run out of the TV truck and look up. PLOP! Your robot drops right into your arms.

Turn to page 68.

"Good shot!" says the TV man. "We'll use it on the news tonight."

A policeman comes by and arrests the junk man for "robotnapping."

Turn to page 41.

Way out at sea, the crew puts up a new flag—with a skull and crossbones!

"PIRATES!" you yell. "Stowaways!" shouts the captain. "All stowaways must walk the plank."

The pirates grab you and your robot. You know your robot cannot swim. You can, but there are sharks out there. What should you do?

If you walk the plank, turn to page 52.

If you try to fight the pirates, turn to page 54.

ABOUT THE ILLUSTRATOR

Illustrator Keith Newton began his art career in the theater as a set painter. Having talent and a strong desire to paint portraits, he moved to New York and studied fine art at the Art Students League. Keith has won numerous awards in art such as The Grumbacher Gold Medallion and Salmagundi Award for Pastel. He soon began illustrating and was hired by Walt Disney Feature Animation where he worked on such films as *Pocahontas* and *Mulan* as a background artist. Keith also designed color models for sculptures at Disney's Animal Kingdom and has animated commercials for Euro Disney. Today, Keith Newton freelances from his home and teaches entertainment illustration at the College for Creative Studies in Detroit. He is married and has two daughters.

ABOUT THE AUTHOR

R. A. Montgomery has hiked in the Himalayas, climbed mountains in Europe, scuba-dived in Central America, and worked in Africa. He lives in France in the winter, travels frequently to Asia, and calls Vermont home. Montgomery graduated from Williams College and attended graduate school at Yale University and NYU. His interests include macroeconomics, geopolitics, mythology, history, mystery novels, and music. He has two grown sons, a daughter-in-law, and two granddaughters. His wife, Shannon Gilligan, is an author and noted interactive game designer. Montgomery feels that the new generation of people under 15 is the most important asset in our world.

For games, activities, and other fun stuff, or to write to R. A. Montgomery, visit us online at CYOA.com

Watch for these titles coming up in the

CHOOSE YOUR OWN ADVENTURE®

Dragonlarks® series for Beginning Readers

"In a world where children have so little autonomy, my children found delight as they were given the choice to create their own adventure. . . . Fun! Fun! Fun!"

— cyoa.com

SEARCH FOR THE DRAGON QUEEN
DRAGON DAY
RETURN TO HAUNTED HOUSE
THE LAKE MONSTER MYSTERY
ALWAYS PICKED LAST
YOUR VERY OWN ROBOT
YOUR VERY OWN ROBOT GOES CUCKOO-BANANAS
THE HAUNTED HOUSE
SAND CASTLE *limited availability*
LOST DOG!
GHOST ISLAND
THE OWL TREE
YOUR PURRR-FECT BIRTHDAY
INDIAN TRAIL *limited availability*
CARAVAN *limited availability*

"My seven-year-old son was captivated by the idea that he could have a hand in guiding a story about having his very own robot. The story lines kept my son reading over and over. Well done!!!"

— cyoa.com

 Purchase online at www.cyoa.com or ask your local bookseller